This Little Pig

JANETTE OKE'S

Animal Friends

This Little Pig

Illustrated by Nancy Munger

BETHANY BACKYARD®

This Little Pig
Revised, full-color edition 2001
Copyright © 1984, 2001
Janette Oke

Illustrations by Nancy Munger
Design by Jennifer Parker

Published by Bethany House Publishers
A Ministry of Bethany Fellowship International
11400 Hampshire Avenue South
Minneapolis, Minnesota 55438
www.bethanyhouse.com

Printed in China

Library of Congress Cataloging-in-Publication Data

Oke, Janette, 1935–
    This little pig / by Janette Oke; illustrated by Nancy Munger.
        p. cm. — (Janette Oke's animal friends)
    Summary: Hiram the piglet is born into a very competitive litter, but they all eventually learn to get along.
      ISBN 0-7642-2448-4 (pbk.)
1. Swine—Juvenile fiction. [1. Pigs—Fiction. 2. Animals—Infancy—Fiction. 3. Farm life—Fiction.] I. Munger, Nancy, ill. II. Title.
PZ10.3.O338 Th 2001
[Fic]—dc21
                            00-011553

Dedicated with love to
Alexander Nicolas Logan,
who joined our family on
December 27, 1990,
a new son for Marvin and Laurel
and a baby brother for Nate,
Jessica, and Jacquelyn.
And to Kristalyn Lorene Oke,
born on February 7, 1991,
daughter of Lorne and Debbie
and baby sister for Katie.
May God bless our time together.

JANETTE OKE was born in Champion, Alberta, during the depression years, to a Canadian prairie farmer and his wife. She is a graduate of Mountain View Bible College in Didsbury, Alberta, where she met her husband, Edward. Both Janette and Edward have been active in their local church as Sunday school teachers and board members. The Okes have four grown children and several grandchildren and make their home near Calgary, Alberta.

CHAPTER
One

I am a baby pig. I'm so young, I don't even know my name yet. I have new brothers and sisters, too. I was sleeping, but someone next to me kept moving around. I opened my eyes to see what was the matter.

"Hey, watch it," I squealed angrily. "You almost stepped on my eye."

"Well, get your eye outta the way," he answered in a real sassy voice.

"My eye is where it's supposed to be," I informed him. "It's your foot that's out of place."

"Quit your—"

But Mother's voice cut in. "There is plenty of room for everyone," she informed us both. "Don't argue. Please. You disturb everyone when you fuss."

The words were firm, but the love in her voice took all of the sting out of them. It was true. I could hear my siblings stirring. It wasn't long before we were all awake.

Mother introduced us to one another as soon as we could keep our eyes open long enough to pay close attention to her.

"I want you to meet your sisters and brothers," she said to all of us. "I will start with the oldest, Othelia."

Mother pointed her snout at a girl who stood slightly apart from the rest of us. The sister squirmed at the attention, seeming real pleased with herself. I recognized her as the one who could do a good job of pushing when it came to the dinner table. But we all said hello, and then Mother went on.

"And this is Tillie—and beside her, Millie."

As I looked at them, I wondered if I'd ever learn to tell them apart. They looked exactly alike to me. We said our hellos again as Mother introduced Higgins and Bee-Bee, too.

"Then we have Hiram."

It took a minute before I realized that Mother was pointing her nose at me. All eyes turned to me, and I felt shy. Then Mother turned and went on with the introductions.

"And this is Hawkins," Mother said with a shake of her head toward the big one.

"The bully," I said under my breath. But aloud I said, "Hello." I was glad to know the name of the one I'd been fighting with. Now I could yell out his name and give him a shove with my shoulder. Maybe he felt the same way. As we all said our hellos, he looked right at me and didn't even blink.

CHAPTER
TWO

The days passed quickly. I became very attached to Mother, even when I wasn't having dinner. She talked to us at times. She would lower her head close to ours, and I could see her soft, brown eyes as she spoke. At first it was very gentle. But as we grew, the words were more direct: hushing us when we got too demanding, scolding us when we argued, and instructing us about the farm.

We slept, scrambled for our next meal, ate hungrily, and slept again. Now and then Mother rolled up onto her feet, shook us all free, and turned to her feeding trough. We heard her eat and drink noisily. Then she would grunt a few times, nose us all aside, and flop down in the straw again. As soon as she was settled, we would all squeal our way to her side and snuggle up against her again.

As we grew, we became more and more curious about our surround-ings. Mother listened to our questions and answered whatever we asked.

"Where is this place?" I asked.

"This is the barn—or, rather, the shed attached to the barn."

"Are we the only ones who live here?" Tillie asked.

I could have answered that. I had already seen some strange creatures stirring about in our shed.

"Oh no," said Mother. "Many animals live here."

"What kind of animals?" asked Othelia.

"More pigs. Cows. Horses. A dog. Cats. Then there are the fowl."

"Fowl?"

"Chickens. Geese. Turkeys."

"Where are they?" asked Othelia, her eyes darting here and there with a frightened look. The thought of so many animals must have scared her.

"In the barn. In the barnyard. Over in the hen house and chicken coop," answered Mother, not one bit concerned.

Just then, the barn door opened, and a young girl came in. Mother lowered her voice and said, "That's the farmer's daughter. She takes care of us. Of all the creatures that live on the farm, she is the nicest one of all."

Mother looked adoringly at the girl. We all watched, too, waiting to see what was so special about the girl.

CHAPTER
Three

Mother did not seem the least bit nervous when the girl made her appearance. We soon learned that we didn't need to high-run to the corner and try to bury ourselves in the straw.

"Good morning, Mrs. White Sow," she said to Mother. She leaned over the pen to scratch behind Mother's ear. Mother grunted her pleasure.

"How are your piglets?" she asked next, still busily scratching behind Mother's ear. "I see they are growing quickly. You must be taking good care of them," she went on, not waiting for Mother's answer.

Then she climbed over the boards that

separated us from the rest of the shed. She headed straight for the corner where we huddled together. To my surprise, she scooped *me* up.

"And how are you, piggy?" she asked me. "I think you are going to make a fine porker. I can hardly wait for you to be big enough to play with."

I was a bit put out with her for calling me piggy. My name was Hiram.

"Daddy says your brother is going to be bigger, and maybe I should choose him for my project. But I like you. You're cuter."

I didn't know what she meant, but I liked the idea of her choosing me. Her soft hands rubbed my sides and stroked my back. Then they moved to scratch behind my ear. Now I knew why Mother grunted with joy whenever the girl scratched her in such a way. It felt just wonderful. I wanted to curl up and fall fast asleep.

Before my eyelids had a chance to close, I was gently lowered to the straw bed again.

"I'll see you tomorrow," she called over her shoulder. "I have to do my chores now."

The door closed behind her, and I stood blinking in disappointment.

Perhaps Mother felt the same way. She turned away from her trough and headed for the straw bed. Flopping down on the softness, she wiggled her nose back and forth in the straw.

"Come!" she called to us. "It's nap time."

We didn't need to be invited twice. We all ran for Mother. Hawkins butted up against me even harder than usual, nearly knocking me off my feet. I gave him a dirty look. Then I noticed the look in his eyes. I knew that he had heard everything the girl had said, and he wasn't happy.

CHAPTER
Four

I knew that I was growing. I could feel my strong body and see my filled-out sides. My legs were longer and faster, too.

As the days passed, I became more and more curious about the shed in which we lived. I spent time sniffing my way around our little home, trying to discover new smells and sights. Hawkins shared my curiosity. If I discovered something interesting, he quickly nosed me aside and took over the investigation.

I didn't like his rude bullying. But there

wasn't much I could do about it except to squeal whenever he threw his weight around. It didn't do much good, because he was still bigger than I was.

Once, when he had forced his way roughly by me, I called angrily after him, "You might be bigger . . . but . . . but the girl says I'm cuter."

He was facing me in a moment, glaring into my eyes angrily. "Don't you ever say that to me again, do you hear? Or . . . or we'll see who's cuter. I'll . . . I'll make you sorry for thinking you're so . . . so great."

I decided not to mention it again, but he couldn't stop me from thinking about it. Whenever the girl came to visit, both of us tried to make her notice us. Whatever her project was, we didn't want the other one chosen for it.

I concentrated on eating. I had heard Mother remark to Higgins that he should be sure to eat well so he would grow big and strong. I figured that meant me, too.

In my dreams I saw myself catching up to Hawkins, and then growing until I was much bigger than he was. I imagined myself towering over him, bullying him into moving aside for me, or just tramping right over the top of him.

Don't tell Mother, but I really loved those dreams. Yet when I opened my eyes, I was still the little brother. No matter how big I got, Hawkins was always bigger.

CHAPTER
Five

We were spending more and more of our time outside. The sun was getting warmer, too. One of our favorite activities was to sleep stretched out in the dirt, soaking up the sun.

I guess one day it got too warm, because Mother decided that it was time to get up. We scattered on the ground as Mother stood—some on our backs, some on our sides, and some lucky enough to land on our feet.

We thought she was taking us inside. But the path that Mother took was wet and muddy, away from the barn.

Ahead of us, I could see a low spot

where dark mud stained the surface of the field. It looked wet and deep—like one could almost get buried in it. I hoped that Mother would see it in time to not step in it.

But Mother was headed directly for the spot.

"Mother," I finally managed. "The . . . the mud."

Just as I choked out the word, something moved. The *mud* moved. I stopped dead in my tracks and held my breath. Mother kept right on walking with all of the litter but me at her heels.

"The mud," I squealed after them. "It's . . . it's alive."

The mud heaved again and up came a head. Then the mouth opened and spoke.

"I wondered how long you would be. It's getting quite warm."

It was the voice of Mrs. Red Sow.

"Yes," Mother replied. "It is. But they needed their rest."

Without even slowing down, Mother walked right on into that deep, gooey mud and shoved her nose into it as though searching out a special place. We all clustered around the edge, afraid that it would swallow her up. Then *plop*, down she went right on her side. The mud flew out in all directions. We had all been splattered. I wanted to turn and run, but I heard Bee-Bee giggle. I forced myself to open my eyes and take another look.

Mother was still there. She hadn't sunk out of sight after all. Her mouth was working as she smacked with satisfaction. Her eyes were closed against the heat and light, and she had a very happy look on her face.

"Ahh," she sighed.

We looked from one to another. We were wondering which one of us would be brave enough to try it first.

CHAPTER
Six

It was Othelia who stepped forward first. Her eyes showed her fear. She took one step, then another. She was already up to her knees in mud. I saw her make a face. I don't think she liked it.

She took another tentative step and frowned again. We all waited.

Suddenly, there was a rush and a splash as Hawkins threw himself forward! He landed with a splattering of mud right against Othelia, sending them both sprawling into the gooey mess.

I had never seen Othelia move so quickly. She was back on her feet in a flash, blinking mud from her frightened eyes and smacking her angry jaws. When she could speak again, she turned to Hawkins, and a scream came from her throat.

"Hawkins," she squealed. "You . . . you bully! You . . . you dumped me." She began to cry.

Mother was on her feet then, grunting out comforting words to Othelia and, in the next breath, scolding Hawkins. By now he was up on his own four feet, blinking away mud and grinning.

"Don't cry," said Mother to Othelia. "The mud won't hurt you. Why, we love the mud—all of us."

Then she turned to Hawkins, and her voice lowered. "Don't push," she said sternly. "Your sister was brave enough to be first. You let her take her time in getting into the Hole."

Hawkins waded out, a grin still on his

face. He looked directly at me and muttered
one word. "Sissy!"

I hadn't set one
foot into the messy
mud in front of me.
And Hawkins knew
it. I was tempted to

hurl myself into the Hole to show him that
I wasn't a sissy. But one close look at the
black stuff was enough to change my mind.
I felt like hurling myself at Hawkins instead.
But seeing his dripping, gooey body
changed my mind about that, as well.
Without a word, I turned and followed my
sisters up to the straw bed.

CHAPTER
Seven

I t wasn't long before we became interested in what Mother was eating. She seemed to enjoy it so much, and it smelled so good.

Hawkins, still being the biggest of us, was the first one to try something from Mother's trough. I don't know how he managed to reach it, but he did. I guess his legs were a bit longer than mine.

Hawkins came away smacking his lips and looking like he was the ruler of the universe. So smug and pleased with himself, he was. It made me even more determined to stretch my way up into that trough, too.

A few days passed by, and I still wasn't big enough to reach. Hawkins kept stealing a bite here and a bite there and grinning from ear to ear. It really upset me, but there wasn't much I could do about it.

One day, as we cuddled up in the straw bed, I noticed Mrs. Red Sow and her family feeding at the outside trough. My stomach rumbled with the desire to join them. Yet, as I watched, it knotted up in fright, too.

I had never seen such pushing and shoving. It was plenty long enough for eight middle-sized pigs, but you would have thought that there was room for only one. They pushed and shoved and squealed and screamed and fought for every mouthful they took.

I trembled as I watched them, and then I thought of something. The outside trough from which they ate was much lower than the one inside where Mother usually took her dinner.

"I'll bet I could reach it," I whispered to myself.

I saw Hawkins' snout twitch in his sleep. I was sure that he smelled the delicious odor, as well, and probably thought that he was only dreaming it.

Carefully, oh so carefully, I wiggled my way out of the straw. As soon as I was on my feet, I started for the food. At the rate those pig fellows were eating, I was afraid I would get there too late.

They didn't even seem to notice me as I stood there and tried to pick an opening. One came when one big fellow, with a thrust of his nose, sent a brother tumbling to the ground. Before the fallen one could get back on his feet, I flung myself directly at the trough.

As if by a miracle, I was able to grab one mouthful before I had to quickly duck out again. It was just as I had thought. The food, whatever it was, was delicious. I backed off a few steps and stood chewing and chomping, smacking my jaws and enjoying myself as I never had before. Now I knew why Hawkins looked so smug.

Eight

It wasn't long before we were all eating
from the trough. And just as we were
getting used to that, we noticed that Mother
and the other larger pigs often rooted
around in the ground and came up with
satisfied looks and smacking jaws.

"What are they doing?" murmured
Othelia.

I shrugged my shoulders. I wasn't sure,
but whatever it was, they seemed to be finding something to eat.

It was Bee-Bee who pushed forward and
dared to ask Mother.

"What are you doing?"

"Eating," Mother said simply.

"Eating? What?" continued Bee-Bee.

"There are all sorts of good things in the ground," said Mother. From the way that she was smacking, we knew that she was right.

"How do you find it?" asked Othelia.

"Just shove your nose in and give a push this way and that," said Mother.

"How do you know what is good?" asked Bee-Bee.

"If it tastes good—eat it," responded Mother.

I cast a glance toward Hawkins. Surely he would be the first to try it just to outdo me. I quickly thrust my nose at the ground with as much effort as I could put behind it. *Whump!* For a minute I saw stars.

"No, no. Not like that," said Mother. "You must push and wiggle and lift. Like this. Watch!"

I wished that she had explained that in the first place.

It took a while for us to catch on. Sure enough, it was Hawkins who was successful first. He wasn't modest about it, either.

"Look!" he cried for everyone to see. "Look! I did it. I did it. I got my nose right into the ground." Hawkins stood with little bits of black earth slowly dribbling down the sides of his nose. He didn't have a thing in his mouth—which was, after all, the purpose of the whole exercise. But he seemed to have forgotten that.

"Good!" said Mother, very pleased with Hawkins' effort. "Now the rest of you try it."

We pushed and wriggled and shoved at the earth with our small snouts. One by one, we raised our heads to squeal when we accomplished the task. The second part of the lesson required actually coming up with something worth chewing. After a few unsuccessful efforts, we were able to do that, as well. I guess each one of us felt very smug and grown-up.

CHAPTER
Nine

"You know," Hawkins bragged to me one day. "I could root my way right out of this yard."

I thought it was just another of his boasts. But if there was a chance that he really could, I wanted to go with him. We had all noticed the vegetable garden outside our pen and were dying to get into it.

"Humph!" I responded, hoping to make him prove himself. "How do you plan to do that?"

"Right under that gate."

I was sure that there had been a time when any of us could have slipped under the gate. But that was when we were younger and didn't know about vegetable gardens. Now we were older and bigger—too big to slip out under the gate.

"Goose did it. Remember?" Hawkins told me.

"Yeah, but that's different. They're allowed to leave the pen. And Goose is smaller than we are. Face it, Hawkins. It just won't work."

"You don't think I can, do you?" he grunted back.

I tossed my head so that my ears flopped and frightened off the two flies that had been buzzing around my head. "No," I said simply. "I don't."

He didn't even answer me—just headed straight for the gate and lowered his snout to the ground. I could see that he was making a little bit of headway.

"You think you're going to dig your way

out?" I teased.

"You'd be smarter to save your breath for digging," Hawkins answered with a sneer and went on with his work.

I had never thought about teaming up with Hawkins before. Suddenly, I realized that he was right. I shouldered up beside him and put my snout to the ground. It was surprising what the two of us could accomplish together. It wasn't long before we had a fairly good-sized hole under the gate. I decided that it was time to see if we could wriggle our way out.

"Let me try it," I urged, pushing against Hawkins. "I'm smaller. Let me see if it's big enough for me to fit."

But Hawkins pushed me aside. "Sure," he said. "You'd go ahead and squeeze your way out and leave me to do the rest of the work myself. Nothing doing. You keep digging until it's big enough for both of us."

I didn't say any more. Reluctantly, I went back to work. Hawkins wouldn't let me get near the hole under the gate until he was sure that it was big enough for him to slip through.

As usual, he went first. I followed, trying to push past him to see what there was to be discovered.

CHAPTER
Ten

We were out! Out of our pen. This was cool. There was so much to see and do, I hardly knew where to start. But then I remembered the vegetable garden, and without waiting another minute, I was off.

Suddenly, there was a loud noise. I whirled around to see what was going on and saw the black-and-white farm dog headed straight for us. Hawkins and I did the only reasonable thing to do. We swung around, stuck our curly tails in the air, and ran for all we were worth.

I headed for the garden still, but this time not to eat. It seemed like a perfect place

to hide. Because of the tall plants and the heavy leaves, I was sure that one small pig could plunge into the growth and be completely hidden from the dog.

Hawkins was going in the same direction. I figured that he must be heading for the same place that I was.

The dog must have figured out what we were doing. My legs moved just as fast as I could make them go. But the dog was able to catch up before we had a chance to duck under the leaves of the rhubarb or into the patch of potatoes.

With a nip to my shoulder, he shouted at me to turn. Without hesitation, I turned. I was in no position to argue my case with Dog.

Faster and faster I ran, squealing for Mother and wishing with all of my heart that I'd had the good sense to stay in my own yard. We had almost reached our hole in the fence when I spotted the dog again. He was coming toward us on the run. He hadn't taken very many steps before he opened his mouth and began his loud barking. It scared us almost out of our skins.

We both ran for our fence. Hawkins got there just a bit ahead of me. He made a dash for the opening. I was right at his heels, ready to duck through before the dog reached us.

I don't really know what happened. Maybe in his hurry, Hawkins had chosen the wrong hole. Or maybe he didn't hit it at quite the right angle. For whatever reason, he got stuck. And there I was with the dog fast approaching and no place to hide.

I tell you, no one could have slept through what happened next. Hawkins was squealing. The dog was yapping. And I was

running back and forth along the fence,
screaming for Mother to rescue me. From
the mud hole came all of the pig family,
screaming and grunting and shouting for us
to get ourselves back to safety.

The farmer and his wife soon appeared,
running toward the commotion. The farmer
fell on his knees beside Hawkins and tried to
hold his squirming body so that the wires of
the fence would not hurt him further. I
could see that Hawkins had already
scratched his back in more than one place.

I heard a few snips and then a scrambling. I looked up in time to see Hawkins go
scurrying into our yard, still screaming at
the top of his lungs. Mother was there to
meet him, and he ran directly to her.

Luckily, I was able to scramble under
the fence without getting caught. As I ran to
the far end of our yard, I wasn't sure that I

wanted to listen to any more of Hawkins'
schemes. My legs were trembling with
fright, and I could hardly catch my breath.
All that I wanted to do was to find Mother
and rest for a long, long time.

CHAPTER
Eleven

Not long after that, the farmer and his daughter came to our pen and looked us over.

"Is it time?" she asked. The farmer nodded.

"Have you decided?" he asked the girl. This time it was her turn to nod.

"Him," she said. She pointed a finger at me.

"The other one's still bigger," the farmer told her, pointing at Hawkins.

I held my breath. I was afraid that she would change her mind. And I did so much want to be the one chosen.

"I know, but I have always liked this

one. And besides, the bigger one has the scars from the scratches on his back and side," said the girl.

I was very thankful that I hadn't gotten myself tangled up in that fence.

Before I knew what was happening, I was being herded through another small door and into a new pen. I expected the rest of the family to follow me, but the door was shut firmly behind me. I was all alone.

I could still see them. I could still talk to them. But I could no longer curl up with them at nap time or join in their squabbles at the feeding trough. In fact, I had my own clean, warm bed and my very own feeding trough. I had the whole breakfast or dinner or supper all to myself.

At first it was hard to get used to. I was

surprised at how much I missed my family. Even Hawkins. Still, I must admit that I felt special. I knew that I was being treated better than the others.

I was given food that I had never tasted before. I loved it. And I was given fresh, clean bedding every day. I was even washed and brushed and petted and pampered. I loved the company of the girl almost as much as I had loved the company of my family.

From next door, my brothers and sisters watched all of the strange happenings in my pen.

"Why all the fussing?" asked Hawkins. "What did you do to deserve all of the special attention?"

I was tempted to boast a bit. I wanted to say, "She thinks I'm cute. Remember? She likes me best." But I didn't try to answer his question. The fact was, I really had no idea why I was getting special treatment—except that she kept referring to her project. But I loved it.

CHAPTER
Twelve

After I was moved into my new pen, strange things began to happen. Some days the girl came with a harness and fastened it around me. To this she clipped a leather strap, and we began to take walks together. It was wonderful to get out into the bright sun and the fresh air, but I hardly had time to notice them.

We walked and paused, turned this way and that way, walked and paused. Sometimes she scolded me. Sometimes she praised me and slipped me a piece of green apple. I soon discovered what it was that she wanted me to do before she offered me another treat. I liked the outings, but I liked the apples even more.

"He's doing great, isn't he, Dad?" she said one day. The farmer was leaning on a pitchfork handle, watching our walking and pausing.

"He is," he agreed. "And he is filling out nicely, too."

"I'll bet he's the biggest one in the litter now," she continued, scratching me behind the ear.

I thought she must have forgotten about Hawkins. He had always been bigger than I was.

"Do you think we have a chance, Dad?" she questioned.

Her father smiled. "He's a nice-looking pig. And you've done a good job with him. Sure, I think you have a good chance."

"C'mon," she said to me. "Let's practice a little bit more."

The farm dog trotted up beside us. I wasn't afraid of him anymore. He never nipped me, and he seldom barked. He just whined softly to the girl.

"What do you think, Rex?" she asked. "Will my pig do well at the fair?"

Rex didn't answer her question. He just licked her hand with a long, wet tongue. But I felt my head swelling. I was beginning to think that I was one pretty special pig.

CHAPTER
Thirteen

All this talk about the fair had me curious. I didn't know what it was, and no one bothered to explain it to me. Was the fair something to eat, someplace to visit, or something to sleep on?

I knew I was about to find out, though, because one day I found myself getting a very special bath. Something was different about this day.

After a lot of grooming and brushing, the girl put me in a special pen. All the family soon gathered in the yard. My pen was lifted into the back of the truck. The farmer and his daughter climbed in, and we were off.

I could see through the mesh across one end of my pen. We drove down road after road. I had no idea where we were going.

After a long time of bumping and swaying, we arrived at a big field. There were many, many buildings and pens, some small and some big. There were also more people and families than I had ever seen before!

The girl bounded out of the truck and stood in front of my pen. "Well, what do you think of the fair?" she asked in an excited voice.

So this is the fair, I thought to myself, a bit disappointed. I had expected something . . . something more special. Something more fitting for a special pig like me.

All around me there seemed to be total confusion. Animals ran about, making noise and kicking up dust. People spoke in loud voices and bumped into each other. Other people stood behind food carts and yelled out to those passing by.

The day was warm, and I was tired. I grew weary of watching all the commotion, so I stretched out on the soft straw for a sleep. Whatever it was I was supposed to do here, I hoped it wasn't going to be soon.

Fourteen

I woke up some time later to an excited voice.

"It's our turn. It's our turn," the girl was shouting. She opened the gate of my small pen and slipped the leash onto my harness.

"Come now," she coaxed. "Be good. You must be on your best behavior."

We walked around together, moving, then pausing, turning this way, then that way. I knew all of the moves perfectly, but I guess she needed to practice a bit more. I didn't mind helping her, as long as she didn't keep me out in the sun too long.

Finally, she seemed satisfied that she

remembered all the moves. We left the practicing and moved over to where several other pigs were also walking and pausing.

I didn't know any of them. They all looked shiny clean and brushed. Some of them even had ribbons around their necks.

"This is where you will be judged," the girl said. Then she placed me just so and stood stiffly beside me.

I looked around at the other pigs. Was I competing against them? But they all looked so big and important! What was I doing here?

There was movement as people strolled here and there and chattered about this or that. I grew more and more nervous. What if I embarrassed myself? What if I forgot something?

The girl must have noticed my nervousness. Every now and then, she leaned over and scratched my ear or stroked my back or just spoke to me.

Soon a little group moved over to us. They asked me to stand and walk, then pause, then turn this way and that way. I did my very best, and before I knew it—it was over. We walked back to our spot.

The small group of chattering people moved along with us, sizing me up from every angle. I was even touched by a hand several times. Then the little group moved on.

Several minutes passed, and it seemed a long time later when the little group came back our way again. One of them stepped forward, said some words, and placed a blue ribbon around my neck.

"We did it. We did it!" the girl cried, hugging me around the neck. Her whole family was there, too, hugging and shouting along with her. "The very best pig in the show—Junior Section," they kept saying.

The very best pig in the show—Junior Section. I didn't understand exactly what all of that meant, but I knew I had been picked as the best. I could feel my chest swell. I could hardly wait to get home and tell my family members, especially Hawkins. I knew that he would be green with envy.

CHAPTER
Fifteen

We left the fair and all its excitement later that day. I was glad to see our barn coming into view. I was even more excited when I spotted our pig pens. I couldn't wait to tell my family about my special day—to tell them about the ribbon and how happy everyone had been that I was the best in the show.

As soon as I was back in my pen, I crowded up to the boards. All my brothers and sisters were waiting for me on the other side.

"Where have you been?" Hawkins demanded. "We thought you weren't coming back."

"I was at the fair," I informed them all with a bit of a swagger. "Remember? I was picked to go."

"Fair? What was it like?"

"It's a place full of people. And animals. And noise. Lots of noise. Everyone was moving about, and dogs were barking, cows mooing, sheep bleating, geese honking—all at the same time."

"It must have been awful," said Othelia.

I grinned. "No. It was exciting. Really exciting. I loved it."

"What did you do there?" asked Millie.

"I . . . I . . . " I could hardly wait to share my great news. I puffed out my chest and lifted my chin higher. "I won a blue ribbon," I blurted out excitedly, sure that they would all cheer my accomplishment.

"A blue ribbon? For what?" asked Hawkins.

"For being the best pig at the fair—Junior Section," I hastened to say. Now I was really sure they'd see how important I was. I watched for their reaction, knowing they would be amazed.

But my news was followed by silence. No one was cheering. Six pairs of eyes stared blankly at me.

"So where is this blue ribbon?" asked Hawkins. My chest returned quickly to normal size.

"The girl has it," I answered.

"I thought you said you won it," said Hawkins.

"I did! That is . . . I did! Honest." Why were they turning against me?

"Then why don't you have it?"

"I won it. Honest. It means that I was the best pig at the fair—Junior Section. The judges said so."

"What do you do with a blue ribbon?" asked Tillie. At least she sounded a little interested.

"I . . . I don't . . . really know," I stumbled.

Othelia began to laugh. "Can you eat a blue ribbon?" she asked me in a teasing voice.

"No," I answered crossly. I was angry that they were spending all their time asking silly questions.

"What do you do with it?" asked Hawkins.

"I . . . I don't know. But the whole family danced and clapped and . . . "

"Hiram," said Othelia. "You are just a pig like the rest of us. Just the same. No different."

"Yeah," joined in Hawkins. "You are a pig like the rest of us. Best pig at the fair—

phooey!"

I had felt proud and puffed up just a few minutes ago, but now I wasn't so sure.

I pulled my snout back from the boards of the pen and retreated to the far corner. I flopped down in the straw, still hearing the jeering and teasing that was coming from next door.

I did an awful lot of thinking. Finally, I came to the conclusion that my family and their opinion of me was far more important to me than I had realized. I had spent all of my growing-up time competing for first place with my siblings. Especially Hawkins. Hawkins had always been bigger, so I felt that I had to be better. I figured that if I finally managed to outdo him, it would make me feel pretty good.

Now I had won best pig in the show. But I didn't feel good at all. In fact, I felt downright terrible. Terrible and lonesome. I was a pig. Just an ordinary pig like the rest of them.

"You are right," I admitted, scrambling over to the boards between our pens. "I am still a pig just like you. We're family—equal. I . . . I was just . . . treated special and . . . and fed special and trained . . . to do the things that the girl wanted me to do. Any of you could have done the same. I'm sorry if I made you feel bad."

There was silence.

"I'm . . . I'm sorry for acting so . . . so cocky about the blue ribbon," I continued. "Please . . . please can we . . . can we forget all about it?"

It was Bee-Bee who spoke up first. "I think it's nice that you won the ribbon," she said frankly. "It should make us all feel a little proud."

Tillie and Millie both lowered their eyes and then looked up to nod slowly.

"You . . . you worked hard," admitted Othelia. "You deserved the award. I guess we were all just a little jealous."

The others nodded in agreement. Even Hawkins.

"Yeah. Let's not compete anymore. I think I like it better when we're friends . . . not just brothers," Hawkins said.

I couldn't have agreed more.

BETHANY BACKYARD®

PICTURE BOOKS

Spunky's First Christmas
by Janette Oke

Spunky's Camping Adventure
by Janette Oke

Spunky's Circus Adventure
by Janette Oke

Annie Ashcraft Looks Into the Dark
by Ruth Senter

Cows in the House
by Beverly Lewis

Princess Bella and the Red Velvet Hat
by T. Davis Bunn

Making Memories
by Janette Oke

Hold the Boat!
by Jeremiah Gamble

Annika's Secret Wish
by Beverly Lewis

Fifteen Flamingos
by Elspeth Campbell Murphy

Sanji's Seed
by B. J. Reinhard

Happy Easter, God!
by Elspeth Campbell Murphy

BOARD BOOKS
by Christine Tangvald

God Made Colors...For Me!
God Made Shapes...For Me!

God's 123s...For Me!
God's ABCs...For Me!

REBUS PICTURE BOOKS
by Christine Tangvald

The Bible Is...For Me!
Christmas Is...For Me!

Easter Is...For Me!
Jesus Is...For Me!

CLASSIC CHILDREN'S STORIES
by Janette Oke

Spunky's Diary
The Prodigal Cat
The Impatient Turtle

This Little Pig
New Kid in Town
Ducktails

Prairie Dog Town
Trouble in a Fur Coat
Maury Had a Little Lamb

NONFICTION

Glow-in-the-Dark Fish and 59 More Ways to See God Through His Creation
by B. J. Reinhard

The Wonderful Way Babies Are Made
by Larry Christenson

Fins, Feathers, and Faith
by William L. Coleman

Series for Young Readers*
From Bethany House Publishers

THE ADVENTURES OF CALLIE ANN
by Shannon Mason Leppard

Readers will giggle their way through the true-to-life escapades of Callie Ann Davies and her many North Carolina friends.

ASTROKIDS
by Robert Elmer

Space scooters? Floating robots? Jupiter ice cream? Blast into the future for out-of-this-world, zero-gravity fun with the AstroKids on space station *CLEO-7*.

BACKPACK MYSTERIES
by Mary Carpenter Reid

This excitement-filled mystery series follows the mishaps and adventures of Steff and Paulie Larson as they strive to help often-eccentric relatives crack their toughest cases.

THE CUL-DE-SAC KIDS
by Beverly Lewis

Each story in this lighthearted series features the hilarious antics and predicaments of nine endearing boys and girls who live on Blossom Hill Lane.

JANETTE OKE'S ANIMAL FRIENDS
by Janette Oke

Endearing creatures from the farm, forest, and zoo discover their place in God's world through various struggles, mishaps, and adventures.

RUBY SLIPPERS SCHOOL
by Stacy Towle Morgan

Join the fun as home-schoolers Hope and Annie Brown visit fascinating countries and meet inspiring Christians from around the world!

THREE COUSINS DETECTIVE CLUB®
by Elspeth Campbell Murphy

Famous detective cousins Timothy, Titus, and Sarah-Jane learn compelling Scripture-based truths while finding—and solving—intriguing mysteries.

* (ages 7–10)

Family Treasuries of
TRUE STORIES
From the Lives of
CHRISTIAN
HEROES

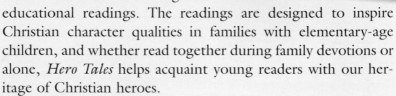

DAVE & NETA JACKSON

H ERO TALES

A Family Treasury
of True Stories
From the Lives of
Christian Heroes

Drawn from the lives of fifteen key Christian heroes, each *Hero Tales* book is a beautifully illustrated collection of exciting and educational readings. The readings are designed to inspire Christian character qualities in families with elementary-age children, and whether read together during family devotions or alone, *Hero Tales* helps acquaint young readers with our heritage of Christian heroes.

 HERO TALES: VOLUME I
Tales include: Amy Carmichael, Harriet Tubman, Samuel Morris, Martin Luther, Dwight L. Moody, John Wesley, and more!

HERO TALES: VOLUME II
Biographies include: Corrie ten Boom, John Bunyan, Watchman Nee, John Newton, Florence Nightingale, Jim Elliot, and others!

HERO TALES: VOLUME III
Heroes include: Billy Graham, Mother Teresa, Brother Andrew, Luis Palau, Lottie Moon, Jonathan & Rosalind Goforth, and nine more.